Flashlight

by **Betsy James**

illustrated by **Stacey Schuett**

Alfred A. Knopf · New York

For Cathy through bright and dark
—B.J.
To Jasper and Nico
—S.S.

our house.

My sister is so little, she goes to sleep anywhere, even in restaurants. She doesn't care if we have to sleep in Grandpa's living room, or if Mom and Dad are far away, in the bedroom down the hall.

But all I can see is dark. That door to the hallway is a cave.

Out of my mouth comes a little crying sound.

Out of the cave comes a bear—but it's only Grandpa. "Did I hear my Mouse?" (My name's Marie, but Grandpa calls me Mouse.)

I rub my head on his warm pajama shirt.

"Dark, ain't it?" he says. "Thought you might like a flashlight."

He puts a heavy shape into my hands, and shows my fingers how to push the switch.

In the all-of-a-sudden light I see his face, and Tibby sleeping.

"Now you're all right," he says. "If you need me, you call."

The flashlight beam follows him back down the hall.

I click the switch. The whole world disappears.

I click it again, quickly, and the world comes jumping back. That forest of legs is the table. That leaning mountain is the chair. Something could hide there.

But wherever I point
the flashlight, the shadows
run away.

There is the cat teapot.

There is the blue bowl
with peaches.

There is the music box
that plays "The Tennessee
Waltz," and there is the
one-eyed horse that in the
daytime I can ride.

The flashlight doesn't look at things all at once, the
way the sun does, but one by one. It's my night eye.

A moth comes.

Back and forth across the beam it
flies in flashes. The window screen is
crowded with whining midges,
bumbling June bugs, and ants with
wings. They love my light.

But I'm the one who chooses when it shines. I can cover it with one hand. Watch!

The flashlight's warm. Fire glows right through my bones.

I can go into dark places, shining.

My sheet is a tent. I'm hunting
treasure. Here are my jewels. There
are bears!

"Tibby!" they growl. "Eat Tibby!"

But I tame them like moths.
"Stay there, you bears!" I say,
and they stay.

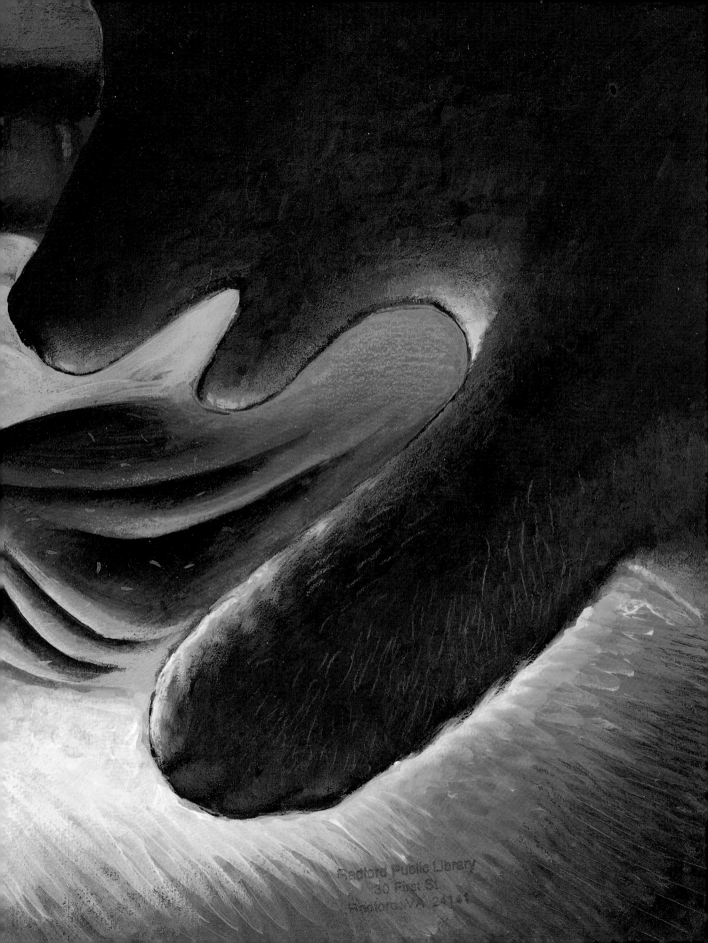

I explore to the very bottom of the bed,

where it's usually just feet.

Through caves and tunnels I crawl back

The living room
is new. This is my
flashlight country.
I make the sun
shine here. I can
make shadows run.
I can boss moths
and bears. I am
the queen of the
night world,
Marie! I can see in
the dark.

I switch off the light.

I switch it on again, but the shadows are back.

They move. Tibby sleeps.

"Grandpa?"

He comes out of the dark, rumpling his hair. "What, Mouse?"

"Nothing. I was making sure."

"Sure."

After he goes, I whisper, "Don't be scared, Tibby. I've got a flashlight."

Text copyright © 1997 by Betsy James
Illustrations copyright © 1997 by Stacey Schuett
All rights reserved under International and Pan-American Copyright Conventions.
Published in the United States of America by Alfred A. Knopf, Inc., New York,
and simultaneously in Canada by Random House of Canada Limited, Toronto.
Distributed by Random House, Inc., New York.

http://www.randomhouse.com/

Library of Congress Cataloging-in-Publication Data

James, Betsy.
Flashlight / by Betsy James ; illustrations by Stacey Schuett.
p.   cm.
Summary: Marie is afraid to sleep overnight in her grandparents' living room
until her grandfather gives her a flashlight so that she can see in the dark.
ISBN 0-679-87970-6 (trade) — ISBN 0-679-97970-0 (lib. bdg.)
[1. Fear of the dark—Fiction. 2. Grandfathers—Fiction.] I. Schuett, Stacey, ill.
II. Title.
PZ7.J15357F1   1997
[E]—dc20   95-33333

Printed in Singapore

10 9 8 7 6 5 4 3 2 1